CHARLIE

and the Cheese and Onion Crisps

CHARLIE

and the Cat Flap

Look out for all the Charlie books!

*Charlie and the Cheese and Onion Crisps
and Charlie and the Cat Flap*

*Charlie and the Rocket Boy
and Charlie and the Great Escape*

*Charlie and the Tooth Fairy and Charlie
and the Big Birthday Bash*

*Charlie and the Haunted Tent
and Charlie and the Big Snow*

For older readers:

*Saffy's Angel
(Winner of the Whitbread Children's
Book Award)*

Indigo's Star

CHARLIE

and the Cheese and Onion Crisps

CHARLIE

and the Cat Flap

Hilary McKay

Illustrated by Sam Hearn

Hodder
Children's
Books

A division of Hachette Children's Books

Contents

Charlie and the Cheese
and Onion Crisps

No Crisps

It was lunch time at school and Charlie and Henry were sitting together. They always sat together because they were best friends. Charlie and Henry had been best friends for five years, ever since they met on

3

the Naughty Bench at Pre-school.

Nobody understood Henry as well as Charlie did, and nobody understood Charlie as well as Henry did. So when Charlie said to Henry, 'You can have my cheese and onion crisps if you want! They give you such a ponky smell!'

Henry understood at once. 'You don't usually mind smelling ponky,' he said. 'Usually you like them the best! You've gone bonkers again, haven't you?'

Charlie smiled and did not say he hadn't.

'Who is it this time?' demanded

Henry. 'No, don't tell me! I can guess! It's the new student teacher that came this morning!'

Charlie's smile got worse than ever, and he gazed across the dining hall at the new student teacher.

'What's her name?' asked Henry. 'I wasn't listening when she said.'

Charlie shrugged. He hadn't been listening either. He didn't think her

name mattered. She was simply the New Miss, fascinating and lovely because she had long red curly hair and a leather thong round her neck with a stone threaded on to it.

'I can't see anything special about her,' said Henry, 'she gets ratty dead easy and she looks like a witch. That stone round her neck is just a normal boring stone.'

'I know. I heard her tell Lulu she found it on the beach.'

'That's not a good reason to wear it round her neck,' said Henry. 'I found a dead seal on the beach once ...'

'You've told me a million times!'

'... A *huge* dead seal ...'

'Seals aren't that huge,' objected Charlie.

'They look much bigger dead than they do in zoos. Parts of it had been chewed or something. It smelled a bit like ...' (Henry glanced into Charlie's lunch box) '... ham sandwiches and a bit like it had died of old age ...'

'I don't know why you're telling me all this *again*!' groaned Charlie.

'I'm just explaining that it definitely wasn't the sort of thing you'd want to wear round your neck ...'

Charlie picked the ham out of his sandwich and pushed it down Henry's collar. A dinner lady caught him ham-handed and sent him to stand by the wall. Henry trailed after him because they were friends and they continued gazing at the New Miss.

'Rubbish shoes,' remarked Henry.

'Girls,' said Charlie, 'only ever look good in very high heels or roller skates. I don't see why they don't just wear them all the time. I would.'

'You'd fall over all the time then.'

'I wouldn't,' said Charlie, rolling his eyes at Henry's silliness, 'because I'd be a *girl*! Dope!'

Henry fished a bit of ham up from under his collar and ate it. He did not bother to argue any more. He knew it would be no good. Falling in love did weird things to Charlie's brain. Now (like countless times before) he would give up cheese and onion crisps, try and teach himself football tricks, spend a great deal of time smiling and leaning against walls, and arrange his hair in unnatural formations of swirls and spikes with hair gel borrowed from Henry's vast hair gel collection.

There was only one good thing about Charlie in love.

'It never lasts long,' said Henry thankfully.

Lunch ended, Henry and Charlie went outside and the New Miss went back to the classroom. Charlie practised football tricks as close to the window as he dared while Henry kept an eye on her through the glass and from time to time said helpfully, 'She's not watching ... good job she didn't see that ... she's still not watching ...'

The New Miss did not survive the
afternoon. First she ruined Art
by handing out paper plates and
demanding they all draw healthy salads
and then she gave out worksheets about

Henry the Eighth with pictures of all of his six unfortunate wives.

'Label the wives and colour them in,' she ordered.

Charlie gave all six red floppy hair and stones round their necks and the New Miss put his worksheet in the recycling bin.

'I hope you are not trying to be rude,' she said.

Charlie, who could be much ruder than that without trying at all, was very offended indeed.

Henry was right; he decided, she did look like a witch.

'I should like to meet someone *perfect*,'
he said as he walked home with Henry,
and he described his perfect girl to Henry.
Henry was not a bit surprised to hear
that she would have floppy hair and sticky
out plaits and her neck would be hung
with interesting things on strings.

Also she would be a whiz on a skateboard or roller blades or very high heels.

'And,' said Charlie, tossing his Art into a nearby bin, 'she will never eat salad!'

'Salad *is* good for you,' said Henry. 'Look at elephants.'

'Yes, look at elephants!' said Charlie. 'They are fat and wrinkly and nearly extinct!'

'I'll tell my mum that,' said Henry, very impressed. 'She's been saying look at elephants and making me eat salad for years!'

'You tell her then,' said Charlie.

'I will,' said Henry, and he did, while Charlie stood around nodding helpfully.

'Look at elephants!' cried Henry's mother, vacuuming around them as if they were furniture. 'Whenever am I supposed to get time to look at elephants, may I ask?' and she shooed them upstairs with an apple and a satsuma each and two tubes of smarties because it was Friday.

They gobbled up their apples and exploded their satsumas and agreed to

save the Smarties for a little bit later
when Charlie would teach Henry the
Truly Amazing Smarties Trick (at which
he was almost perfect). After that they
gelled up their hair into gravity defying
banana-scented spikes with Henry's
latest hair gel (Tropical Fruits Extra

Tropical Fruits
Extra firm
hold!
BANANA!
GEL.

Firm Hold) and Henry described *his* perfect girl to Charlie. And she was going to be so very, very rich that she would insist on giving Henry at least a million pounds just to save her the bother of looking after it.

And then she would go and live on the other side of the world.

The moment Henry took delivery of the cash.

'Admit she sounds perfect,' said Henry smugly.

Charlie said she didn't sound real.

'Neither does yours,' said Henry, and then they went back into the street to check their spikes would stay up in the wind, and Henry said, 'Crikey!'

Because there she was.

Charlie's perfect girl.

Coming down the street with Charlie's big brother Max.

2

Quite a Lot of Smarties

The Perfect Girl was in school uniform, and she made it look like the coolest clothes in the world. Her huge school uniform shirt almost covered her tiny school uniform skirt. Her school uniform tie had been transformed into a belt. A denim backpack swung from one shoulder and two sticky-out blonde plaits bounced from under a heap of blonde floppy hair. Around her neck were silver chains, strings of shells and a large blue stone on a leather thong. She did not walk, she glided and spun as if she was on wheels.

She *was* on wheels; she wore white wheelie trainers.

She floated along the pavement, sometimes a little ahead, sometimes backwards talking and shaking her plaits, but she kept coming back to Max.

'It is NOT FAIR!' wailed Charlie.

It never was fair with Max. He was four
years older than Charlie, and it seemed
to Charlie that he had been born with
Charlie's share of good luck as well as
his own.

Max was very nearly a
teenager and so tall he looked
even older than that. He was
good at everything. He could
whistle through his fingers,
raise one eyebrow and juggle
with a football. He could
swing from the crossbars of the
swings in the park, do running
dives into the swimming pool
and ride a bike with no hands. He grew

so quickly his clothes did not get time to wear out and then Charlie, who never seemed to grow at all, had to wear them for ever.

There were times when Charlie could hardly bear his big brother Max.

Max and Charlie's perfect girl had paused on their way. She had pointed to a notice fastened to a lamp post, and they had read it together. Charlie and Henry saw the Perfect Girl smiling and nodding. They saw Max shrug and move away. They were getting closer and closer but they did not seem to see Charlie bobbing up and down on the pavement.

In fact, they both kept glancing backwards.

'What'll I do to make her notice me?' wailed Charlie and almost at once found the answer in his hand.

The Truly Amazing (Nearly Perfect) Smarties Trick.

The Truly Amazing (Nearly Perfect) Smarties Trick had another name: Drinking Smarties. The performer held a tube of Smarties high above his open mouth and drank them as they poured. It was a wonder of breathing and swallowing and timing.

Max and the Perfect Girl were only a few steps away.

Charlie pulled open his Smarties tube, and tipped back his head.

Rattle, rattle, rattle, went the stream of Smarties into Charlie's open mouth, and vanished.

It really was spectacular.

It was a five second multicoloured miracle. Not a single Smarties missed. It was Charlie's most successful performance ever.

Henry applauded, Max looked disgusted and the girl on wheelie trainers who had missed the whole thing asked, 'What?'

'Me!' squeaked Charlie. 'Watch properly this time!' and he grabbed

Henry's tube of Smarties.

'OY!' shouted Henry, but too late.
Charlie was beginning the whole trick
all over again.

It should have worked but it didn't.
Henry's shout put Charlie off so that
the whole drinking and breathing and
timing thing was ruined.

Charlie choked like an explosion
and a volcanic eruption of Smarties
shot from his face and showered his
astonished audience.

'What a waste! What a waste!' yelled
Henry, scurrying round gathering up his
property.

'OUUFFF!' went Charlie, and hurled
another rain of Smarties into the air.

'Stop it! Stop it!' complained Henry

furiously. 'He'll die!' announced the Perfect Girl. 'He's choking! He'll die!'

'He'll not,' said Max grumpily.

'He's my brother. I've seen him do it thousands of times before. He's just disgusting.'

'WHARRRGGGHHH!!!!!' said Charlie, erupting again.

'Do something!' the girl ordered Max, so Max picked Charlie up, hoisted him upside down and shook him. A stream

of Smarties tumbled
out like pennies
from a piggy
bank and Charlie
stopped choking
and went suddenly
boneless.

'That was the
most amazing
thing I ever
saw!' said the
Perfect Girl,
gazing round at
the constellations of Smarties still
ungathered by Henry. 'How many do
you think he ate? Shouldn't someone be
taking care of him?'

'I just did,' said Max, lowering

Charlie not very gently on to the
pavement and beginning to move
quickly away.

'Does he do it *often*?' asked the Perfect
Girl, hurrying after him.

'Yes. Quite.'

'They're both gathering up Smarties
now!'

'Probably going to eat them.'

'The one that's your brother is smiling

at me. I love his hair! He must have done it himself ...'

Max grunted and walked a bit faster. They were quite far away now but the voice of the Perfect Girl came floating back, laughing and clear.

'He really is kind of cute ...'

Charlie suddenly came alive with happiness.

'It worked!' he cried, punching Henry joyfully. 'Did you hear what she said? Cute! She said cute! How about that?'

'Oh fantastic,' said Henry sourly. 'Are you sitting on any more Smarties?'

'Loads!'

'I'm having all mine back!'

'OK. I only borrowed them.'

'Borrowed them and swallowed them!'

'Just for a minute,' said Charlie soothingly. 'What did you think Henry, when you heard her say I was cute?'

'I thought she was bonkers,' said Henry.

Skateboard Tricks

'So,' said Charlie to Henry on Saturday morning. 'What'll I do next? Now that I've got her thinking that I'm cute and everything?'

'Why don't you ask Max?' asked Henry. 'He should know. He likes her too.'

They were in the park at the time, the little green park just along the street from their houses. Their mothers had decided that this summer they were allowed to be there on their own. After all, it was so close that you could see it from the windows of Charlie's house, and the road in between was very quiet.

'They ought to be safe,' said Charlie and Henry's mothers.

Charlie and Henry did not feel very safe that Saturday morning. They were taking turns with Henry's skateboard which they had recklessly oiled before they came out. Oiling had transformed it. Before only two of the wheels moved at all. Now all four of them spun at a touch. Charlie and Henry hardly dared step on it.

'Maybe we should gunge it up again,'

suggested Charlie. 'And Max doesn't like her. He's not bothered about her at all. He told me.'

'Ho!' said Henry disbelievingly, and looked across the park. Gemma was in the little one's playground, carefully pushing someone's toddler on one of the

baby swings. A group of Max's friends were taking turns to vault a bench. Max was all by himself, not quite in the little one's playground because no footballs were allowed there, but very nearby. He was doing fantastic football tricks. He could bounce the ball from his knees to his head, catch it on his shoulders, slide it down his back, and hook it up with his foot all in one easy movement.

It was lovely
to watch,
but no one was
looking except Charlie
and Henry.

'He's
got his
hair gelled
up just like yours,' said
Henry. 'And he's looking at
her just the way you looked at the New
Miss on Friday.'

'The way I looked at who?'

'The New Miss,' said Henry. 'Floppy
hair! Awful shoes! Half a dead seal
round her neck!'

'Oh her,' said Charlie, stepping
very carefully with one foot on to the

skateboard, 'Look, I'm doing it Henry!
I'm balanced!'

'Make it move then!'

Charlie scooted forward the
smallest amount possible and stayed
triumphantly upright.

'Woo hoo!' he sang, glided at least six

inches and waved boldly to Gemma.

Gemma smiled and waved back.

This was too much for Charlie. His arms flailed in frantic windmill circles and he toppled over backwards into a flower bed.

Gemma's eyebrows flew up and she raised a hand to her mouth.

'I'm all right! I'm all right!' cried Charlie, bouncing to his feet and racing across the grass to the swings with Henry stumping along behind him. 'I'm actually very tough, aren't I Henry? I really like your

pink hat! D'you mind if I look at your trainers? Did you know you've got my favourite sort of hair? I heard what you said about me yesterday, you know!'

'What did I say?' asked Gemma.

'You said I was cute!'

'Did I?'

'You know you did!' said Charlie, attempting a somersault over a baby swing and landing at her feet.

'Well,' said Gemma (who had delicious dimples both sides of her mouth), 'so you are!'

And she reached down with both hands and pulled

him up again.

A football shot like a comet past
Charlie's left ear, close enough for him
to feel the whoosh of air as it passed.
A flying figure sped across the grass,
leaped on to Henry's abandoned
skateboard, rode it in a
tremendous
screeching curve
down the path,
jumped the three
steps down to the gate
(landing perfectly, crouched
and balanced like a cat) and
vanished beyond the bushes between
the park and the road.

Moments later the skateboard came
sailing into view.

It landed with a flump on the grass.

'Max,' said Henry, 'does not think
that Charlie is cute.'

Bmq x Chaz

A few minutes later Charlie arrived home and bounced up the stairs to the room he shared with his brother. There was a big sulky lumpy bump on the top bunk that belonged to Max.

'There you are!' said Charlie in a pleased happy voice. 'I looked for you everywhere downstairs. Did you see me with Gemma?'

The bump on the bed lashed out with a sudden foot.

'I'm going to make her a card to say Happy New House because she's just moved to a new house. So is it OK if I borrow your new felt pens because I don't know where you hid them?'

The bump growled.

'And some of your card if you don't mind and could you fold it in half because I can never do it neat enough?'

The bump gave a big sigh.

'And then I'll go away.'

The bump on the bed rolled on to the floor and turned into Max. Max pulled his sleeping bag out of the bottom of the wardrobe and reached his new felt pens down from the top. He took a sheet of cardboard from his school art folder. He folded the card very neatly in half.

'That's perfect,' said Charlie.

Max opened up the top of the sleeping bag and slid the felt pens and card inside. After that he picked up Charlie and scrunched him into a ball and dropped him into the sleeping bag too. He shook it so that all the junk settled at the bottom and he twisted the top closed. Then he heaved the whole bundle

on to his shoulder, carried it out of the
room and dropped it down the stairs.

Charlie tumbled and rolled down the
stairs, across the hall, out of the open
front door and into the garden where his
mother and Gemma were talking over
the gate.

'... Saving up for a karaoke machine,' he heard Gemma say he slowed down. 'I love little kids! *Goodness*!'

'Hullo Gemma!' said Charlie, crawling out of the sleeping bag.

'What *happened* to you?' asked Gemma, and at the same time Charlie's mother demanded, '*Now* what have you done to Max?'

'Nothing,' said Charlie, glaring scarily at his mother and smiling even more scarily at Gemma, and marched off to make his card. On the front he wrote Happy New House over a very bright picture that used every one of

Max's new felt pens. Inside he added the other thing he wanted to say. Under a large red glowing heart with sharp black arrows shooting through it he wrote:

B m9
X
Chaz

It looked so good that he took it round to Henry's house for Henry to admire.

'How's she going to know what it means?' asked Henry. 'Chaz? What's Chaz?'

'Chaz is just a cool way of saying Charlie,' explained Charlie.

'And what's be-M-nine?'

'Be *mine*,' said Charlie. '*Be mine*, it says.'

'Then X marks the spot?'

'*NO!* That's a … oh, never mind!'

'I only asked,' said Henry primly, 'because if it's not X marks the spot it looks a bit like it could be a kiss so you might want to change it. How are you going to give it to her?'

'I thought you could.'

'*Me?* Why me?'

'Because,' said Charlie, 'you're my best friend.'

That was true, Henry was Charlie's best friend.

'She's in the park right now, with someone's kid. She loves little kids. I heard her telling my mum.'

'Oh all right,' agreed Henry and he stomped away with the card to find Gemma.

She was see-sawing a borrowed
toddler and looking very bored indeed.

Henry, who quite liked babies offered,
'D'you want me to go on that see-saw
with him? I could give him dead good
bumps.'

'No thanks.'

'Push him on the swings?' suggested
Henry, and passed him a packet of

bubblegum sweets so he could help himself. The toddler stuffed a fistful into his mouth and overflowed with pink drool.

'You musn't give them stuff!' protested Gemma, as she grabbed him and hung him over the bin.

'Sorry. I came to bring you this.'

'What?' asked Gemma, plucking off the toddler's hat, mopping his face with the pompom and plonking it back on again.

'Oh, a card. Thank you! Is it from you?'

'NO!'

'Who then?'

'You have to work it out.'

'Who gave it to you to give to me?'

she asked cunningly.

'Ah ha!' said Henry, now at the top of the climbing frame. 'Look! No hands!'

The toddler looked in admiration and began climbing frantically towards him.

'Just let go!' said Henry encouragingly. 'That's right! Now the other one ... or are your legs too short?'

The toddler tumbled into Gemma's arms and knocked her off her wheels.

The roars were tremendous.

'Legs too short,'

diagnosed Henry suddenly losing
interest, and went home.

Charlie, watching the whole thing
through the landing window, had sighed
with satisfaction when he saw Gemma
open her card.

'Now she knows,' he said.

The Only Thing Max Couldn't Do

Max was behaving very oddly.
He was moaning about his
trainers.

And trying on all his T-shirts.

He even cut slits in his new jeans and
carefully frayed the edges.

'Mum will kill you,' said Charlie,
watching.

Also he spent a lot of time just staring

at himself in the mirror.

'What do I look like from the back?' he asked Charlie once.

'You look the same as you do from the front,' said Charlie. 'Only without a face.'

A day or two later Charlie came in from the garden and heard music playing upstairs. When he crept up to investigate, there was Max.

At first Charlie thought he was doing exercises to music.

And then he thought he was trying to wriggle out of his shirt to music.

Or to reach an itch to music.

And then he realized that what Max was doing was trying to dance.

That was very odd, because Max did not approve of dancing. He always made excuses, saying things like, 'I have leg ache/ I have homework/ My bedroom needs tidying/ I am watching this programme/ Reading this book/ Very busy with this cat ...'

Or sometimes, simply, 'I wouldn't be seen dead ...'

Not a bit like Charlie, who together with Henry had been livening up dance floors since he was three years old. Charlie and Henry loved discos. They would dance with anyone, sing along to any song, and consume anything left lying on the refreshment table.

While Charlie was watching Max his favourite song in all the world came

on the radio and he could not resist
joining in.

'*HEY!* (Hey!) *You!* (You!) *Get Off of
My Cloud*!' sang Charlie, doing big
stomps, and playing air guitar with his
eyes shut and leaning backwards which
he knew, because Henry had told him,
looked cooler than the coolest of cool.

'*Don't hang around 'cos
two's a crowd!*'

Suddenly the music
was switched off, and
Max was asking,
'How do
you do it?'

'What?' asked Charlie, opening his eyes.

'Did you see anyone and copy? Did someone actually show you? Is that the sort of stuff you and Henry do when you go to discos?'

For a few moments Charlie's head whirled. Always in the past it had been Charlie asking Max a million questions about something that seemed to everyone else to be as easy as breathing.

'I only asked,' said Max, 'because I may have to go to a disco and I think when I am there I may have to ... may have to ... may have to ...'

'Dance?'

'Yes, and you seem to be able to! Anyway, you don't go red and you don't keep stopping ...'

Was this really Max? wondered Charlie. The Max who had taught him to blow bubble gum bubbles, ride a bike, slide the fireman's pole in the park and make squeakers out of blades of grass. Was he joking?

It was Max, and he wasn't joking.

Charlie felt suddenly very old and wise and successful. He felt like the grown up big brother, with Max for the useless little one.

For the next half an hour he tried very patiently to teach Max how to dance.

It was very, very hard.

'You have to move your arms and legs,' said Charlie. 'Pretend you are playing the drums! Or a guitar like me!

Sing the
words! Make
them up if you
don't know them!
Try not looking
at your feet for
a bit!'

'Anyway,' said
Charlie, encouragingly
(although nothing
had improved
and it seemed,
incredibly, that the
only thing Max couldn't do was the
only thing he, Charlie, could), 'they'll
play slow dances at the end. They
are much easier. You just rush to the
prettiest girl in the room (you may have

to push a few people out of the way), and say "I'm dancing this with you" and grab her and don't let go ...' Then Max, who was not scared of ghosts, or heights, or any ride at the fair, Max who would fetch a ball from anyone's garden, jump into any depth of water and had once actually spoken in French to a French person, Max the bravest of the brave, looked utterly terrified.

'Grab them?' he asked.

'Yep.'

'What if they won't come?'

'Pull harder.'

'I mean, what if they say "No!" '

'They never say no,' said Charlie, 'they are grateful, Max!'

Max's Big Night Out

'Guess what my brother Max is doing tonight!' said Charlie on Friday night as he and Henry walked home together.

'Bashing you up again?'

'No.'

'Trying out for the England team?'

'Not yet.'

'Not the fourteen Weetabix challenge?'

'No, he's still stuck on twelve. After that he chokes.'

'Give up then.'

'Going to that disco.'

Henry snorted in disbelief.

'He is too! He's going back from school with his friend Greg and they're getting changed and going together. I helped him choose what to wear.'

'You!'

'Yes. AND I taught him how to dance like we do.'

'What, all our pretend guitar playing and everything?'

'Yep.'

'Can he do it?'

'No.'

Henry smirked.

'But it doesn't matter because I've told him all about slow dances and all that. And how to get a girl.'

'What girl?'

'Yes well, he wouldn't tell me that.'

'Gemma.'

'Not Gemma,' said Charlie. 'He doesn't even like Gemma! He doesn't even think she's pretty! He told me.'

'She is though,' said Henry.

'Gemma,' said Charlie sternly, 'is mine!'

They had reached Henry's gate. Charlie opened it for Henry like he was twenty-one and Henry was six. This made Henry very mad and he said, 'I can open my own gate *thank you*, and

as a matter of fact I saw Gemma before
you did.'

'What?'

'I may ask her to go out with *me*,'
said Henry, deliberately being as
aggravating as possible. 'If Max doesn't
want her and you're too scared!'

'I'm not scared.'

'Ask her then! I dare you!'

'I will.'

'When?'

'When I want to.'

'Ha! You won't! Double dare!'

Charlie marched off down the street,
pushed open the door of his house and
vanished inside. The telephone rang.

'Double dare with knobs on!'

Charlie slammed the phone down and

went to fume in his bedroom. After a while his mum came and found him.

'We have a problem,' she said. 'What am I going to do with you this evening, with your dad working late and Max out and me with my yoga class? I suppose I will have to take you with me.'

She groaned.

Charlie groaned too because he did not fit in very well with his mother's yoga class.

'Last time you said never again,' he reminded her.

'Yes, well I often say never again and end up doing it,' said Charlie's mother, 'and by the way Henry has just telephoned with a very strange message. He said to tell you Yellow Knobs.'

Charlie growled, grabbed a handful of lime-flavoured hair gel, rubbed his hair into lime-flavoured tentacles and dashed out of the room.

'Where are you going?' shouted his mother.

'To see a girl.'

'What girl?'

'Gemma.'

'That's a very good idea,' said Charlie's mother, but Charlie had already disappeared.

'Yellow Knobs to you,' he said to Henry, some time later. 'Please don't offer me any cheese and onion crisps or anything ponky like that because I have a Big Night in with Gemma. She is coming over for pizza and then we are watching a DVD!'

'Oh!' exclaimed Henry jealously, 'Oh, it's not fair, having pizza without me! I never have pizza without you. I bet it's pepperoni as well! What DVD are you watching?'

'I'm not telling you because you'd be upset.'

'I may have fallen in love with Gemma too!' shouted Henry. 'I *did* see her before you did!'

'But,' said Charlie, shaking his lime-flavoured tentacles very annoyingly, 'did she see you? Anyway, it's your fault! You dared me!'

'OK,' said Henry. 'Now I'll dare you something else then! I dare you to ask her to marry you!'

'What?'

'Double dare! With ...'

'Of course I will,' said Charlie. 'No problem!'

Charlie's Big Night In

O h, thought Charlie, later that
evening, Gemma is *lovely*!

She and his mother had met at the
front gate; Gemma had come in as his
mother went out. She had glided right
up to him, kicked off her wheelies, and
given him a delicious, bubblegum-
scented hug. While he tried out her
wheelies she had sat on the doorstep

and painted her toenails blue. They ate
the pizza on the doorstep too. Sharing a
pizza with Gemma, Charlie found, was
a very different experience to sharing
with Henry or Max. There were no cross
words about which was the biggest slice
or who had the most pepperoni.

'I don't really like pepperoni,' said
Gemma, and flicked hers into the
bushes. She didn't eat her crusts either,
and she daintily picked off all the
mushroom too. After her second slice
she left the rest to Charlie. He finished
it while she hummed dreamily and told
him all about the karaoke machine she
planned to buy.

After the pizza Gemma ate three
low fat yoghurts because she was on

a diet and Charlie didn't, because he wasn't, and then they settled on the sofa together to watch the DVD.

'In real life,' said Gemma, nodding at the swashbuckling captain of the pirate ship, 'he looks a lot like you!'

'Like me?'

'Definitely. With the right make-up

you'd look just like him. I'll show you if
you like.'

'When? Now? I've got a pirate hat!'

'Come on then!' said Gemma.

It took a while, and a lot of Charlie's
mum's make-up, but it was worth it.

'See!' said Gemma when they were
back on the sofa again with the DVD
running, and the lights turned low.
'Told you so! Exactly like him,
except for the hair.'

'I'll grow my hair,'
said Charlie
huskily,
'Gemma?'

'Mmm?'

'When I'm sixteen how

old will you be?'

'Twenty.'

'Do you want to marry me then?'

'Yeah, all right,' said Gemma.

'Wait till I tell Henry!' said Charlie.

'That was the easiest ever!'

'Easiest what?'

'Nothing,' said Charlie, putting an arm round her.

'Dead cute,' said Gemma.

Then everything was ruined.

Bash! went the front door and it was Max.

Stamp! Stamp! Stamp! went Max down the hall, crashed into the living room and flicked on the lights. Charlie, comfortably slumped against Gemma

and looking exactly like a pirate hero
except for his hair, blinked in surprise.

'Hiya!' said Gemma in a very little
voice.

'OH!' exclaimed Max. 'YOU!
YOU'RE HERE! I MIGHT HAVE
KNOWN! I MIGHT HAVE KNOWN!
GOODBYE!'

'He's a bit weird,' said Charlie, and
he tried to snuggle back down again but
the magic was gone.

'I'd better go,' said Gemma, looking
at her watch. 'Two hours ... two and
a half ... call it three ... I'll just write a
little note ...'

'You're not really going?' pleaded
Charlie.

But she was. She was pulling on her

wheelie trainers and pushing a little pink note in his hand. She rushed out of the house so fast she bumped into his mum coming in. She called, 'Bye Charlie darling!' and vanished.

The evening was over and it was Max's fault and Charlie marched upstairs to tell him so.

Max was face down on his bed and he was fuming.

'... .learning that horrible dancing ...' Charlie heard, '... putting that gunk on my hair and being scared all day! And it cost two pounds! Two pounds to be tortured! And it was her idea! It was all her idea! Hanging around and hanging around and waiting and waiting! She *said* she'd be there! She promised! And in the end I had to go up to her two stupid friends and they thought I was asking them to dance and I had to explain that I wasn't and then do you know what they said?'

'What?'

'THEY SAID SHE'D GOT A LAST MINUTE BABYSITTING JOB!'

'Oh.'

'AND IT WAS YOU!'

'Me?' said Charlie, 'Me? Are you mad? 'Course it wasn't me! I've been with Gemma the whole time ...'

And then he looked down at the pink paper he was holding in his hand.

And unfolded it.

It was very pretty. She had dotted her 'i's with little tiny hearts.

Babysitting

Three hours @ 3.50 an hour
                                    10.50
He has been very good and
I think he had a lovely time
Gemma

'AAARGGHHH!' yelled Charlie, flinging the hateful pink paper on the floor and jumping on it with both feet. 'Rotten girl! Her and her wheelies! Her and her plaits! Babysitting! Do I look like a baby?'

He stared at Max, fists clenched and raging, with rivers of pirate make up

AAAARRGHH

pouring down his cheeks.

Max stared back.

'STOP LAUGHING! IT'S NOT FUNNY!'

'I'm not laughing,' said Max, and he wasn't. He knew too well how Charlie felt.

'What'll I tell Henry?' snuffled Charlie, and buried his head in his arms. He was suddenly very tired of being in love.

Then Max took charge, like he always used to do in a crisis.

'Wait there!' said Max.

'He saved my life!' Charlie to Henry the next morning. 'Max did. When I fainted ...'

'Fainted?'

'... with sadness and he saved my life by wafting crisps round my head till I revived ... cheese and onion. They're making me better. This is the fourth bag I've had since last night. She's mad, you know?'

'Gemma is?'

'Guess what she said when I asked her to marry me?'

'What?'

'She said, "Yeah all right"'

'She's mad,' agreed Henry.

'Blue feet she's got and she won't eat pepperoni. Low fat yoghurt, that's what she likes.'

'Yuk!'

'And my mum says she either can't count or can't tell the time ... anyway, we're over her, Max and me, and we're going swimming after school tonight. Max said he'd take me ...'

'Oh!' said Henry jealously.

'And he said you can come too, if your mum says yes.'

'She'll say yes,' said Henry, skipping with pleasure, 'because she likes Max. She's says he's responsible. And grown up. Grown up and responsible! Can you drink crisps like you can Smarties?'

'No,' said Charlie, 'but I can balance them on my nose and lick them off with my tongue! Max showed me how last night.'

'Cheese and onion?'

'Any flavour!'

'Sounds a bit ponky!'

'Who cares about ponky?' asked Charlie.

'Not Max and me!'

Charlie and the
Cat Flap

Four Days Before the Big Sleep

Charlie and Henry were both seven years old, and they were best friends. They were best friends, and they quarrelled all the time. They argued at school. They squabbled at birthday parties.

They nearly always had to be separated on school trips. Their friends said, 'Charlie and Henry have been like that for ever!' and took no notice; but their teachers called them The Terrible Two. 'Double Trouble!' agreed Charlie and Henry's fathers.

Their mothers said,

'You boys ALWAYS end up quarrelling!'

One Monday morning, Charlie's big brother Max asked if he could stay with a friend for the night on Friday and his mother said he could. This would mean there would be an empty bed in Charlie's bedroom. That Monday afternoon, Charlie and Henry ran out of school to where their mothers were both standing moaning about them and Charlie asked, 'On Friday night, can Henry come for a sleepover?'

Straight away Charlie and Henry's mothers said,

'No!'

'No,' they said. 'We haven't forgotten the last time!'

The last time Henry's father had had to get dressed at two o'clock in the morning and take Charlie home because Charlie said he could not bear listening to the way Henry breathed for one moment longer.

'He is copying my breathing!' Charlie had complained furiously. 'Every time I breathe, he breathes! He has been doing it ever since you took away his

Super Soaker Water Squirter! And what has happened to my Itching Powder and my two dead flies? That's what I want to know!'

So Charlie had been taken home, and Henry's Super Soaker was banned for a week. But the Itching Powder and the two dead flies turned up safe and sound in Henry's bed, where Charlie had put them, and Charlie and Henry soon forgot all about their quarrel. They were astonished when their mothers reminded them. They looked at each other and they put on their Sad Little Boy faces and then they tried again.

Charlie said to his mother: 'You let Max have sleepovers but you won't let me!'

'You like Max better than me!'

'He's your favourite!'

'It's not fair!'

And Henry said to his mother: 'At least Charlie has Max! I have no brothers or sisters and I am fed up with living in a house just with grown-ups.'

Their mothers made moaning sounds but Charlie and Henry did not stop.

They said: 'We never quarrel!'

'Charlie likes it when I hit him.'

'Henry likes it when I push him over.'

'We only argue a bit.'

'I don't argue,' said Charlie.

'How can you say that?' asked Henry. 'You argue all the time!'

'Just because I don't agree with every single word you say!' said Charlie.

'Argue argue argue,' said Henry, sticking his thumbs in his ears and waving his fingers rudely at Charlie. 'Moan moan moan!'

'You think you are so clever!' said Charlie, grabbing at him. 'You are not half as clever as you think you are!'

'You are not a quarter as clever as you think you are,' replied Henry, dodging behind his mother.

'You are not a millionth!' shouted Charlie.

'You are not a quarter of a millionth!' said Henry.

Charlie was not very good at maths and he could not think of any amount smaller than a quarter of a millionth to say Henry was not as clever as, so he did not say anything. He stared up at the sky as if he did not care.

Henry came out from behind his

mother and stuck out his tongue to
show that he had won.

'Ha!' shouted Charlie, and jumped on
Henry and tipped him on to the ground.
It was always very easy for anyone to
tip Henry over. He did not seem to be

properly balanced.

Charlie sat down on top of Henry and Henry flung his arms about and bashed Charlie on the nose. It started to bleed at once. Charlie's nose always bled at the smallest bump. It did not seem to be very well made.

All this arguing and wrestling and nose bashing had taken less than two minutes.

And Charlie and Henry were still best friends at the end of it, but their mothers did not understand that. Henry's mother jerked Henry to his feet and said, 'Now say you are sorry! Look what you've done to poor Charlie!'

Charlie's mother pushed a handful of tissues on to Charlie's nose and snapped,

'Sit still until it stops!'

'It is you who should say sorry! Bumping down on poor Henry like that!'

Then both mothers exclaimed together,

'And you two are supposed to be friends!'

Charlie and Henry stopped asking if they could have a sleepover for the rest of that afternoon. But they agreed to start again the next morning (which was Tuesday). Patiently, maybe a hundred

times, they asked the same question:
'Why can't we have a sleepover?' Also
Charlie said how his mother liked Max
more than she liked him, and that it was
not fair. And Henry said how tired he
was of living with just grown-ups, and
that it was not fair.

It was very hard work for Charlie
and Henry, but in the end it worked.
On Wednesday afternoon their
mothers gave in and said, 'Oh all right!
Anything for peace and quiet! But this
will be your Last Chance Ever!'

Two Days Before the Big Sleep

Charlie and Henry planned the best sleepover ever. They made an agreement:

No Itching Powder, No Dead Flies and No Super Soakers to be squirted at the ceiling in order to make surprise indoor rain.

'We'll look for ghosts,' said Charlie.

'That's a good idea,' said Henry. 'And

we'll have a midnight feast.'

'Brilliant!' said Charlie.

It felt very strange saying 'Good idea!' and 'Brilliant!' to each other, but it was all part of Charlie and Henry's plan. They knew their sleepover would be cancelled if they began quarrelling, so for the next two days they were very polite. They did not fight at all, at least not where anyone could see them.

'It won't last,' said Charlie's mother. She was in a very gloomy mood because the sleepover was happening at her house, but Henry's mother (who was planning a trip to the cinema with her phone switched off) was much more cheerful. She said, 'Perhaps Charlie and Henry are beginning to grow up. At last.'

Then they both said, 'Wouldn't it be lovely!'

It sometimes seemed to Charlie and Henry's mothers that Charlie and Henry were taking an awfully long time to grow up.

Charlie and Henry spent all their pocket money collecting food for the midnight feast. They bought salted peanuts, strawberry bootlaces, cheese triangles, Coca-Cola, chocolate M&Ms and curry-flavoured crisps. They hid all these things in the bottom of Henry's

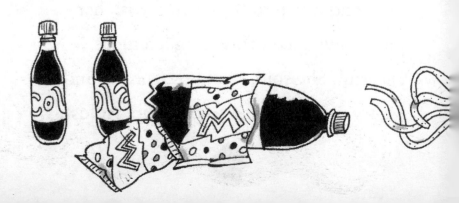

sleeping bag. Henry had carried his
sleeping bag round to Charlie's house as
soon as their mothers gave in and said
the sleepover was allowed. Since then
it had been kept in Charlie's bedroom
in the bottom of the wardrobe that he
shared with Max.

Charlie and Max had bunk beds.
Max had the top bunk and Charlie
had the bottom. Max would never
let Charlie have a turn in the top
bunk because sometimes Charlie had
accidents at night.

'And what if it dripped through?'
Max said. 'And I was underneath!
Horrible!'

Max did not like the idea of Charlie's
sleepover. He said,

'You'd better not touch any of my
stuff up here?'

'And you can tell Henry from me that
he's to leave my skateboard and my
bike alone this time! I wish he wasn't
sleeping in my bed! I hope he doesn't do

what you sometimes do!'

Charlie pretended not to hear.

'Well,' said Max gloomily, 'I suppose he's got a good thick sleeping bag!' He lifted Henry's sleeping bag out of the wardrobe, discovered the bulge in the bottom, and tipped it upside down.

'Those are our midnight feast supplies,' said Charlie proudly, as salted peanuts, strawberry bootlaces, cheese triangles, chocolate M&Ms, curry-flavoured crisps and bottles of Coca-Cola tumbled on to the floor.

'Crikey!' said Max, even more gloomily. 'If you eat that lot you'll both be sick for sure.'

Charlie ignored that too.

'Still,' continued Max, 'maybe Henry

won't be here long enough to eat it! Didn't Mum promise his mother she'd take him home the minute you started fighting?'

'Yes, well, we won't be fighting!' said Charlie. 'And we won't be sick either! So ha ha! We're going to stay awake all night and look for ... ghosts!'

'You two would be scared stiff if you saw a ghost!' Max laughed.

'We wouldn't!' Charlie said. 'I wish we really could.'

'You be careful what you wish for!' said Max, and in the middle of the night Charlie remembered those words.

The Big Sleep: Eight O'Clock Till Ten O'Clock (at night)

Max left, and Henry arrived with a big square bag. Henry's mother had packed Henry's bag very carefully with everything he could possibly need. When she was not looking Henry had swiftly unpacked it again. So Henry had not brought pyjamas or slippers or washing things or anything like that.

Instead he had brought his hamster
in its cage. It took up the whole bag.
Henry lifted the hamster cage up on to
Max's bed and said, 'I thought I could
borrow stuff off you!'

Charlie didn't mind that at all. He
got out a pair of his own pyjamas for
Henry, and found a toothbrush he could
use in the bathroom. After Charlie
had sorted out Henry's pyjamas and
toothbrush he suggested
that they go for
a treasure hunt
through all Max's
drawers and boxes
in search of Interesting
Secret Stuff. They
treasure-hunted

for a long time, but they did not find
anything because Max had guessed this
might happen and he had packed up all
his Interesting Secret Stuff and taken it
with him. Then they made Lego tanks
and had a battle which got noisier and
noisier until Charlie's mother came in
and ordered, 'Bed!'

Henry grumbled a bit about his

pyjamas as they got ready for bed. He said they were pink but Charlie explained they were pale red. Henry didn't say anything about the toothbrush (at the time).

When they were both ready, they went downstairs to say goodnight to Charlie's father and mother.

'Goodnight,' said Charlie's father. 'And remember, if there is any bother I will come and sleep on the floor and I warn you, I snore like a camel, don't I Charlie?'

'Yes,' said Charlie proudly, and Henry said, 'I bet you've never heard a camel snore!' So Charlie said, 'How would you know what I've heard snore?'

Charlie's mother said hurriedly, 'Night-night, boys, sweet dreams, don't talk too long! Are you wearing Charlie's pyjamas, Henry?'

'Yes,' said Henry. 'Mine got left at home. Do you mind?'

Charlie's mother said she didn't mind a bit. She said that as long as he and Charlie did not spend the night quarrelling about camels Henry could wear anything he liked. This was rather a silly thing to say, because as soon as Henry was back in the bedroom he put on Charlie's plastic suit of armour, and the shield and the sword belt and the sword. Then he clanked up the ladder to Max's top bunk where his sleeping bag was already unrolled, and lay down beside his hamster cage. 'Pass me the bow and arrows, please, Charlie!' said Henry.

'No I won't!' said Charlie. 'First you moan about my pyjamas, then you grab my suit of armour and now you want my bow and arrows!'

Charlie got out of his bunk and

picked up the bow and arrows himself. Then he climbed on top of his chest of drawers and shot Henry as he lay in bed.

Henry said in a sad quiet voice, 'I don't mind if you hurt me but please don't frighten my poor little hamster.'

'You only said that to make me feel bad,' said Charlie, fitting another arrow to his bowstring.

Henry did not reply. Instead, with great difficulty, he struggled out of the suit of armour and threw the pieces one by one at Charlie's head. Charlie fired his last arrow and made a rush for the top bunk, intending to pull Henry out and dump him on to the floor. From downstairs came a sudden voice.

'Are you boys behaving up there?'

'Yes!' shouted Charlie and Henry, letting go of each other.

'Nearly asleep?'

'Nearly,' they called, diving under the covers and lying down flat.

'Shall I come up and see?'

'No, no, no!'
yelled Charlie
and Henry with
their eyes tight shut.

For a long time the room was very quiet. And it was very dark.

In the darkness Henry murmured, 'Charlie!'

Charlie nearly jumped out of his skin. 'What?' he asked.

'What if we heard footsteps coming louder and louder up the stairs and then suddenly the door burst open with a huge bang and cold air rushed into the room and a great black shape towered over us and we saw a green light all around and heard the sound of screaming like in Harry Potter?'

'I don't know,' said Charlie, not at all keen on thinking very hard about this idea.

'I only wondered,' said Henry, 'because it's gone very quiet downstairs and I think something horrible has happened to your mum and dad and it's going to happen to us next and I'm sure I saw the door move. Watch!'

Ten O'Clock Till Midnight

Charlie watched the door and watched the door. He watched until his eyes hurt. All he could see was a grey shape, against a slightly lighter greyness, but it seemed to him that Henry was right, and that now and then it did move.

Henry moaned, 'I hate your rotten sleepover!'

That made Charlie mad. 'Big moaning baby!' he hissed.

'If you're so brave, why are you whispering?' demanded Henry. 'Why don't you do something useful? Like shut the door.'

'Because I don't want to,' said Charlie.

'Oh yes!' said Henry. 'I bet you're scareder than me!'

'Scaredy cat!'

'I'm not!' said Charlie, and to prove he wasn't, he bounced out of bed, closed the door properly, and began barricading it with all the biggest things in the room, his skateboard, his beanbag and, balanced on the top, his enormously heavy and rattly box of Lego. Then he

snapped off the light and marched back
to bed.

'Now you will be safe, poor little
Henry,' said Charlie in a very kind
voice.

Henry sighed and rolled over and got

his legs twisted up in his sleeping bag and announced, 'I need to go to the bathroom!'

'You can't! I'd have to move all my stuff!'

'Well, I do.'

'I don't care. You'll have to wait till morning! Think about something else! When shall we have our midnight feast?'

'Midnight, of course,' said Henry. 'I don't know if I can wait till morning.'

'Of course you can! Do you think it's nearly midnight?'

'No.'

'Why not?'

'Because my light-up watch says half past ten.'

'Oh,' said Charlie crossly, because

he had not got a light-up watch, and anyway was useless at telling the time. 'Ages till midnight. We'd better go to sleep for a bit.'

'I can't. I can't get to sleep.'

'Count,' advised Charlie. 'Count yourself scoring goals. Max told me that. It works.'

Henry lay uncomfortably beside his hamster cage and tried it. He dressed himself up in a red and white football strip, cut bright green grass into perfectly patterned squares, filled the largest arena in the world with cheering fans, added a background of ten magnificent red and white players not quite as good as himself, an opposing team in green and yellow, a terrified goalie facing his charge (a goalie who looked exactly like Charlie), and kicked relentless penalties one after another with a ball that left a trail of sparks in the air like a comet's tail. Of course, with each goal the crowd went crazy, and even the opposing team couldn't help but cheer. In fact, as Henry drifted

off to sleep, everyone (and there were thousands, not to mention all the TV viewers) was having a wonderful time except for the opposing team's goalie, who would not admit he was frightened.

Suddenly there was the most enormous sound in the world. And a bright light and screaming. The screaming was Charlie. And Henry, waking from a deep sleep, was aware of a spreading warm dampness.

'Charlie, stop screaming!' cried Charlie's mother. 'It's only me! I am so sorry!

I only thought I would just peep in! I had no idea … Look at this! Lego everywhere! I'm sorry I woke you up,

Henry! Go back to sleep!'

The light went off again and Henry became drowsily aware of Charlie, grumbling to himself as he collected Lego in the dark and rebuilt his fortifications.

'Crikey, that made an awful noise!' murmured Henry as Charlie clambered back into bed.

'I know,' said Charlie. 'I nearly wet the bed!'

'I think I did!'

'You did?'

'I think so.'

'Want me to fetch Mum?'

'No. What'll I do?'

'Nothing,' said the experienced Charlie. 'It'll go away soon. It sort of disappears. I don't know why.'

'OK,' said Henry and sighed with relief, and then he asked, 'How do you know?'

Charlie did not reply. He already felt he had said too much. Instead he started

to snore, and the more Henry said, 'I
know you can hear me! And I know you
know what I mean!' the more he snored.
So eventually Henry gave up. He went
back to counting goals again, slightly
damper than before, but on the whole
much more comfortable. Charlie's
snoring became part of the roar of the
crowd. Henry fell asleep.

Midnight Till Two O'Clock
(in the morning)

Henry was asleep, but Charlie was wide awake. He was sure he could hear something. Something alive, padding around the bedroom. Something sleek and black. A restless whisper that circled the bed. He did not know what time it was.

Charlie was too scared to move or

make a sound and he had never felt so
lonely. Henry was no comfort at all.
The person Charlie wanted most in the
world was Max. Max was scared of

nothing in the world. Not even ghosts.

Now Charlie was remembering what Max had said, when he, Charlie, had wished to see a ghost.

'Be careful what you wish for!'

The out-of-sight patch of blackness that was pacing the room seemed to come a little closer as Charlie remembered Max's words. Charlie's skin prickled and his heart thudded. He tried to breathe silently. He wondered if whatever-it-was knew where he was. And did it know that he was awake? And that his name was Charlie? And that he would do anything, promise anything, give anything – if only it would agree to get Henry instead of getting him.

It was right beside him now.

Charlie closed his eyes and waited to faint, and in the middle of his terror he thought how utterly unfair it was that of all the wishes he had ever made this one should be the only one to come true.

Then it jumped.

It jumped right past Charlie and up on to Henry's bunk and landed with a rattle on the hamster cage.

Charlie laughed aloud in relief.

The thing that he had thought was a ghost was Suzy, the cat. She had finally located where the delicious smell of hamster was coming from.

'Yrrummmm!' said Suzy very happily.

'No Suzy!'

Charlie scrambled out of bed and on

to the bunk-bed ladder and grabbed in
the dark. Henry yelled and woke and
sat up with a jerk that shook the cage
and overbalanced Suzy. She fell on to
Charlie, and Charlie fell on to floor
and they landed together in a yowling,
struggling heap. Moments later the

bedroom door was flung open and the
Lego trap collapsed for the second time
that night.

'What is it?' moaned Charlie's
mother, her hair all on end and
Charlie's father's dressing gown
clutched around her, inside out. 'Oh!

Suzy! Suzy, you bad cat, whatever are you doing in here? Give her to me, Charlie, I'll put her outside. Are you all right, Henry?'

'Is that the cat that ate Charlie's hamster?' demanded Henry.

Charlie's mother made unhappy, don't-ask-me-horrible-questions-at-two-o'clock-in-the-morning noises, caught Suzy, and backed painfully over the Lego to the door.

'Is it?' asked Henry, extremely fiercely.

'I shall close your bedroom door and put her outside in the garden and put the catch on the cat flap so she can't get back in,' said Charlie's mother, speaking as soothingly as she could between the pain of walking on Lego

and an armful of scrabbling cat. 'Go
back to sleep, boys!'

She closed the door carefully behind
her and Charlie and Henry sighed with
relief because she had not noticed the
hamster cage.

'That was so funny!' said Charlie,
laughing.

'Funny!' exclaimed Henry. 'Funny!'
and he leant over
the side of the
bunk bed,
grabbed
a double
handful of
Charlie's
hair and
tugged.

'That's for inviting my poor little hamster for a sleepover with a cannibal murdering cat!'

'I didn't invite your poor little hamster!' said Charlie, pulling away. 'You brought it yourself!' And he laughed again and lay on his bed with his feet pushing very hard at the underneath of Henry's mattress, so that it tipped alarmingly.

'I didn't know you'd still got that cat! Stop pushing my bed! S'not funny!'

'It is!'

Henry swiped as best he could below the bunk with his pillow.

'Missed!' said Charlie, choking with laughter, and pushed even harder.

Henry leaned dangerously far over the

bunk rail and caught one of Charlie's legs. Charlie kicked and they both fell on to the floor. The bedroom door crashed open again and this time it was Charlie's father. His eyes were screwed nearly shut and he was wearing Charlie's mother's dressing gown, which was covered in peach-coloured frills.

'Ouch!' yelled Charlie's father, as he fell over the skateboard and landed on the Lego.

'What the de ... What the bl ... What on earth ...'

He switched on the light, caught sight of himself in the mirror, and switched it off again.

'I give up!' he groaned. 'I'm much too old for performances like this. I'm going

back to bed!'

Henry and Charlie went to bed too,
very quietly in case he decided to change
his mind and come back and sleep on
the floor, as he had threatened to do.

Henry said, 'Doesn't your dad know

any proper swearwords?'

'Yes,' said Charlie loyally. 'He knows thousands! You wait till morning when he's properly awake!'

The house became quiet again. Charlie fell asleep, and Henry nearly fell asleep. Then he remembered something.

'Charlie!' he whispered.

'Mmmm?' groaned Charlie.

'We've got to eat that midnight feast!'

'We will,' mumbled Charlie.

'When?'

'Soon,' said Charlie, after a long, long pause. 'OK?'

There was no reply except a snore.

'Oh well,' said Charlie, and very soon he was snoring too.

Two O'Clock Till Four O'Clock
(in the morning)

Henry's hamster was a very lazy animal. Also he was used to living with Henry, who was a bumpy, noisy sort of person to live with. So the arrival of Suzy the cat on to the top of his cage had not even caused him to turn over in his sleep. But between two and four o'clock in the morning he was in the habit of getting up and running very fast and excitedly in his little green exercise wheel. It made a screeching, rattling sound because it needed oiling. He also liked to chew the bars of his cage very hard. Henry's

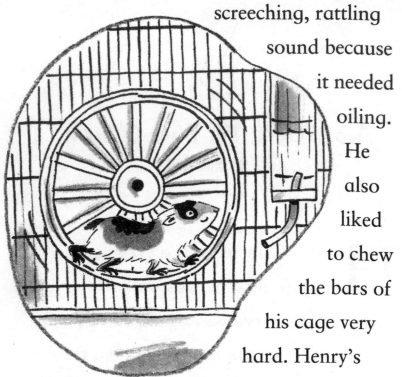

mother said it sounded just like the drill that men use to make holes in roads, but really it was not as bad as that.

However, it was still loud enough

to wake up Charlie and Henry. They woke up as bright and alert as if they had just had ten hours' sleep instead of less than one. They discovered that they were both very hungry, and told each other what a good time it was to have a midnight feast.

'It's brilliant,' said Henry. 'Your mum

and dad must be so exhausted by now that hardly anything could wake them up!'

Later on this turned out to be true.

Henry climbed down into Charlie's bunk and they got out the salted peanuts, the strawberry bootlaces, cheese triangles, Coca-Cola, chocolate M&Ms and curry-flavoured crisps, and they ate the lot. All except for one bit of cheese triangle, which they gave to the hamster.

'Max said we'd be sick,' remarked Charlie. 'Do you feel sick?'

Henry sat for a while in silence to check the way he felt and then said, 'Not really. Do you?'

'No,' said Charlie, after checking

carefully, and he added, 'Max doesn't know everything!'

It was the first time in his life that Charlie had realized this. The idea made Charlie feel good. It made him feel fine and frisky.

The room was no longer dark. It was nearly four o'clock in the morning and because it was midsummer, dawn was not far away. Outside, a bird was beginning to sing. Charlie pulled back the curtain. The garden looked all green and silvery-grey and cool and empty.

'Let's go outside,' said Charlie.

Before Henry's mother had left Henry at Charlie's house she had told him to be good. And so far, he thought, he had been. But now he had a feeling that

sneaking out into the garden at four
o'clock in the morning would not be
being good at all.

Charlie said, in a very good little
boy's voice, 'It would be much nicer
for my mother if we were sick outside
instead of in here.'

'I do feel a tiny bit sick!' said Henry at
once.

'Well then,' said Charlie solemnly, 'we
ought to go outside, Henry.'

'Yes, Charlie,' said Henry, just as
solemnly. 'I think we should.'

So Charlie and Henry went barefoot
and silently down the stairs, feeling that
in all ways they were doing the right
thing.

They were very sorry to find that the

kitchen door, the door that led into
the garden, was locked. The key was
nowhere in sight. Charlie and Henry sat
on the doormat beside the cat flap and
thought and thought.

Afterwards, neither Charlie nor Henry
could remember which of them it was
who said, 'Suzy is a big cat.'

It was a big cat
flap too, homemade
by Charlie's father,

who was very clever at making things. It had a catch on it which could be moved so that it only opened one way. You could have it so that if Suzy went outside she could not get back in again, or so that if Suzy came into the house, she could not go back out again. Or you could leave the catch off altogether, so that Suzy could come and go as she pleased.

That night, Charlie's mother had fixed the catch so that after Suzy had been shooed out through the cat flap she could not come back in again.

'Suzy is a big cat,' said whichever-of-them-it-was.

Then they had a short tussle on the

doormat about who would go first
and Henry won.

Henry stuck his head out of the
cat flap, and then one arm, and then
(wriggling sideways a bit) the other
arm. After that, it was easy for the rest
of him to get through. Charlie followed
seconds later.

Four O'Clock Till Six O'Clock
(in the morning)

It was wonderful in the garden. It was not dark at all any more. The grass was cool and wet with dew, and very slippery to bare feet.

Charlie and Henry played skids on the grass until their pyjamas were soaking wet with dew, and striped from top to bottom with green grass stains and

mud. They agreed that everyone who did not come out and play skids on the lawn at five o'clock in the morning was crazy. Charlie was perfectly happy, and Henry was almost perfectly happy except for one little thing. One tiny little thing that had been at the back of his mind, bothering him, since bedtime.

'Charlie,' he said. 'Where did you get that toothbrush from that you lent me?'

Henry said this standing at the end of the lawn. Charlie took a run and skidded towards him, sweeping his feet from under him so that he toppled like a skittle. Henry always did fall down very easily, but it still made him mad. So he bumped Charlie's head, which of course made Charlie's nose bleed. Then they were both mad, and Charlie would not answer Henry's question.

'I know it was not new,' said Henry, when he had asked his question three or four times more, 'because it wasn't in a packet and anyway it didn't taste new.'

'How did it taste?' asked Charlie, interestedly.

'Old,' said Henry.

'Oh,' said Charlie, and he seemed to

choke for a while, and then he said he was cold and he was going to go back to bed.

This time the cat flap was very, very hard to open. However, at last Charlie managed to force it far enough for him to get his head through. And one arm, but not the other.

All the time he was doing this Henry was demanding, 'Where did that toothbrush come from?' and saying how old it had tasted. The more Henry

thought about it, the older it seemed to him that the toothbrush had tasted.

At about half past five in the morning Charlie became completely stuck in the cat flap. The catch was bent from Charlie's forcing, so the cat flap was jammed half-open. Henry was no help at all. He just kept on and on about the toothbrush. So at last Charlie started shouting for help.

He could not shout very loudly, stuck on his stomach halfway through a very tight cat flap. After several minutes of calling, his parents still had not come down to rescue him. Henry had been right when he said that they must be so exhausted that hardly anything would wake them up.

Charlie was exhausted too. He said to Henry, 'Ring the doorbell.'

'What?' said Henry.

'Ring the doorbell,' repeated Charlie, 'and that will wake up Mum and Dad and they'll come downstairs and get me out.'

Henry said he would only ring the doorbell if Charlie told him where the toothbrush had come from.

'You don't really want to know,' said Charlie, which of course made Henry want to know more than ever. So at last, after a lot of arguing and promising and bargaining, Charlie agreed to tell him. And Henry agreed to ring the doorbell straight after.

Then they fell into complete silence.

'Go on then,' said Henry at last.

'It was my grandma's,' said Charlie.

'WHAT!!!!' yelled Henry, and he ran around the garden with his tongue hanging out, shaking his head and roaring, and then he licked handfuls of grass, and after that he came back and demanded furiously, 'Which grandma?'

'Ring the doorbell!' begged Charlie.

RRAAARGH!

'Which grandma?' shouted Henry.
'The big hairy one or the one you only
let come at Christmas?'

'The one we only let come at
Christmas,' said Charlie. 'Now ring the
doorbell!'

Then at last Henry did ring the
doorbell. But before he did it he gave

Charlie the most enormous stinging wallop on the part of him that was still sticking out of the cat flap.

Six O'Clock in the Morning Onwards

Charlie's father and mother were very surprised and furious when they saw where Charlie was. Charlie's father said he had a good mind to leave him there, and just use the front door from now on.

'Good idea,' said Charlie's mother, and started to go back to bed, but then she said, 'but I can't be going right round by the front door every time I want to hang the washing out.'

So they decided to rescue Charlie after all. His father unscrewed the bent catch and pulled him through the cat flap. They would not let Henry follow, even though he tried to. They let him in the ordinary way through the door.

Charlie's father and mother were not a bit sorry for Charlie, even though he was very sore, and covered in mud and blood and grass stains. They were not very polite to Henry either. Both boys were sent upstairs for a bath and a shower.

'Not a bath or a shower, a bath and a shower,' said Charlie's mother.

'This has been the second worst night of my life!'

She sounded so fierce that they did not even dare ask which had been the first worst. They did not dare to complain either. They crawled upstairs in silence, but when they were in the bathroom Henry caught sight of Charlie's grandma's toothbrush. It made him groan and moan and drink a lot of bathroom water out of the tooth mug.

'Sorry,' said Charlie to Henry.

Then they had a look at the bright red hand print that was glowing on Charlie's bottom. Henry had done that, and he had meant it to hurt, and he could see that it did.

'Sorry,' he said to Charlie.

By the time they came out of the bathroom, very clean and scrubbed looking, Charlie's father had gone to work. And Charlie's mother was quite calm, even though she had now seen the state of Charlie's bedroom, which was more or less covered in Lego and hamster cage sawdust and the remains of the midnight feast.

'Well at least you seem to have stopped quarrelling!' she said.

This surprised Charlie and Henry, who were best friends and thought they hardly ever quarrelled.

Another surprising thing happened when Henry's mother came to collect Henry.

Henry's mother asked (in a very worried voice), 'Well, how did it go?'

'I suppose,' said Charlie's mother, carefully not looking at Charlie and Henry, 'I suppose they could have been much worse!'

Charlie and Henry's eyes met over the breakfast table, and their jaws dropped open in surprise. Looking back on the night, they themselves really could not see how they could have been much worse.

So then Henry's mother said, 'How good! Then perhaps Charlie could come for a sleepover at our house next Saturday!'

Charlie and Henry now waited for Charlie's mother to tell the truth. This did not happen.

'Yes,' said Charlie's mother, very eagerly. 'Yes he could! That would be lovely!'

'He could bring his school things and stay for the whole weekend if you like!' suggested Henry's mother.

Charlie and Henry shook their heads in disbelief, and they thought that even if they lived to be as old as their mothers, they would never understand the ways of grown-ups.

'That would be wonderful!' said
Charlie's astonishing mother, and she
shooed the boys outside and began to
make coffee for herself and Henry's
mother. Henry's mother watched in
astonishment as she poured milk into
the coffee jar and then tried to push the
kettle in the fridge.

'Gosh, sorry!' said Charlie's mum. 'Bit
sleepy!'

Henry's mother thought of the

coming Saturday night and felt suddenly frightened.

Outside in the garden things were much more cheerful. Charlie had just tipped Henry over. Henry was making grabs for Charlie's nose. It looked like they were fighting, but of course they were not.

They were perfectly happy.

They were best friends.

WANT MORE CHARLIE?

READ MORE OF HIS ADVENTURES

 in

CHARLIE

and the Big Snow

Max's Fault (I)

Charlie was seven years old when the big snow came. It was almost the first time in his entire life there had ever been enough snow to make a snowman. The only other time it had happened he had not been allowed out because he was ill.

He had caught the illness from his big brother, Max. Even now, a year later, he had not quite forgiven Max for this.

However, at last it had happened again. Charlie woke up and found that the bedroom he shared with Max was filled with clear cold light. White splodges patterned the window glass. The sky looked close and grey.

Snow! thought Charlie as he scrambled out of bed, and then he thought, Nobody bothered to tell me.

Charlie's father, who was always the first to be up, would already be on his way to work. His mother was in the shower; Charlie could hear the water running. Neither of them had bothered to shake Charlie awake and tell him that it had snowed at last.

That did not surprise Charlie very
much, because after all they were
grown-ups and did not have any sense.
But it seemed to Charlie that Max
should have woken him. Max was
nowhere to be seen.

It takes a monster
to know a monster!

MONSTER + HOSPITAL

Join grumpy Sylvie, bossy Carolyn,
clever-clogs Tom and disgusting Dylan,
the most monstrous children in school,
as they are tasked with curing monsters
of mysterious and revolting illnesses.

www.hodderchildrens.co.uk

Hodder
Children's
Books

MAMMOTH ACADEMY

Neal Layton's classic, lovable mammoths, Oscar and Arabella, are off to school and there's always trouble around the corner at The Mammoth Academy!

www.hodderchildrens.co.uk